SCARRED

DOUGLAS STRAIT

Contents

Chapter 1

The New Neighbor

I t is an early spring morning during the month of May, in an upscale neighborhood where pristine lawns abound. Alone U-Haul van winds along a residential street called Odysseus Drive. The occupant in the driver's seat is Grant Ziegler, a fifty-year-old white man of average build and looks. He is alone in the truck, with a car in tow behind it.

The van approaches a two-story home where a black man with earphones on, Tony Carson, also fifty years old, rides a lawn mower, around a lawn that is the most pristine of them all. He is somewhat large, muscular and with tiny scars around his eyes.

Grant slows the van to a stop and stares at Tony, studying his face. Finally, Tony sees him. He removes the headphones, and shuts off the mower.

"Can I help you?" Tony calls out.

"Yes sir," Grant replies. "I seem to be lost. Can you tell me where 13811 Odysseus Drive is?"

"Down the street a bit and around the bend," Tony explains as he points.

"Ah. Thank you." Grant starts to leave in his van, and then takes a good look at Tony's home. He notices a woods with sparse trees behind the backyard which is open. There is no fence around the backyard Vaguely, through the trees, is the back of an abandoned shopping center. Satisfied, Grant drives on.

Tony pays little attention to the new neighbor, but makes a mental note to get acquainted the first chance he gets.

Behind Tony, the front door opens and a black woman walks toward him with a tall glass of lemonade. This is Gigi. She is the same age as Tony, a little plump, but still retaining much of her younger looks.

"I thought you might need some refreshment," she says to him.

Tony grasps the glass in large hands and takes a long drink of it, nearly emptying the glass while Gigi looks at the U-Haul van heading down the street.

"Who was that?" Gigi asks.

"New neighbor. He was asking for directions to his house. You'd think he would know that."

"Maybe the winding streets confused him."

"Maybe."

Tony hands the glass back, then gets off the mower and pushes it toward the garage. At the garage, Tony scrutinizes his lawn. A prideful smile comes across his face, then he thumps his chest like a gorilla. "Hey, yo," he cries out.

Tony pushes the mower into the garage as Gigi follows.

The garage is large and well organized, large enough to accommodate three cars, but there are only two. One is a sharp looking SUV and the other, an older sedan. When the mower is pushed into the corner, Tony turns and notices a black boy walking down the sidewalk, headed toward their lawn. He knows what's coming. The kid is sixteen and has no manners.

The teenager, Stephen, eats from a potato chip bag and listens to an Ipod. Casually, he throws the potato chip bag onto Tony's lawn.

"Hey!" Tony calls out. Stephen doesn't hear him. "Hey!" Tony shouts louder.

Stephen continues to walk on, not hearing over the music coming through his earbuds.

Tony runs after him.

"I'm talking to you, boy!" Tony says definitively.

Finally, Stephen hears him. He takes the earbuds off.

"What?" Stephen asks.

"You pick that up!" Tony points at the potato chip bag.

"You pick it up."

"You threw it on my lawn!"

"I didn't throw nothin' on your lawn."

"I saw you!" Tony is becoming livid. He gets close. "Pick it up! Now!"

"Hey, get outta my face, old man."

This is the part that Tony has encountered in the past with this kid.

Stephen puts the earbuds back into his ears and walks away.

"You come back here?"

Stephen flips him the finger and keeps walking. Mad as hell, Tony grabs the potato chip bag, storms back toward his garage and slams it into a trash receptacle.

When Tony reenters the garage, Gigi is patient.

"You shouldn't let them upset you like that," she explains. "It's just paper."

"Just paper?! I don't want someone trashing my yard every time they walk by!"

"Kids do those kinds of things." Gigi remains calm.

Tony starts to relax. "Some kids. Not all." He finishes the glass of lemonade. "I'm going for a walk." Tony hands the empty glass to Gigi and heads for the sidewalk.

Tony walks about three-quarters of a mile around a bend to Grant's new home. He notices that it's a brand new one-story ranch style structure, also with the sparse woods behind it. Strips of grass are piled on one side of the house. Grant, wearing work gloves, unloads a refrigerator from the U-Haul van with a hand truck. Tony strides up the driveway.

"Hi, I'm Tony," he begins.

Grant removes the gloves and shakes his hand. "I'm Grant."

"I wanted to welcome you to the area," Tony says.

"Thank you."

"Can you use some help?"

"Sure. I can get the fridge in," Grant explains. "Bring the boxes in the truck to the back and we can transfer them into the house from there."

"Will do."

Grant stops the refrigerator before the garage, then opens the door with a remote. Tony climbs into the truck.

"You looked like you were alone," Tony calls out from inside the truck. "It's a tough job by yourself."

"I could do it, but, it'll get done quicker this way," Grant answers.

"Around here, the neighbors all try to stick together," Tony states.

"Sounds like a good neighborhood to live in."

Grant takes the refrigerator into the garage while Tony moves boxes to the back of the truck so that they can be grabbed easily.

He stops and watches Stephen walk by with a white boy that he's seen before. His name is Brian, Tony seems to remember, and he's the same age as Stephen, sixteen.

"You lookin' at somethin'?" Brian calls out to Tony.

"I'm looking at you. What does it look like I'm looking at?"

There's a history with these boys. Tony scowls at the boys as they grin back. Grant returns and sees Tony's expression.

"Those boys aren't bothering you, are they?" Grant asks.

"The one did a little while ago," Tony tells him.

"It can't be that bad. You looked like you wanted to kill somebody."

"I work on my yard for hours. Days. It's my pride and joy. And that black kid comes along and throws his trash on my yard."

Grant laughs. "That would bother me too, I guess. But, nowadays, it's African-American. Not black." Grant grabs the boxes and stacks them on the hand truck. "Grab something and come on in."

"Back in my day, it was black and not colored," Tony tries to explain. "Or Negro. Black's still in."

"Yep," Grant quips. "The right thing to say might be the wrong thing to say, but you might as well say the wrong thing because it'll be the right thing eventually, huh?"

When they enter the garage, Tony chuckles at the comment.

Upon following Grant across the garage floor with a box in his arms, Tony notices a set of golf clubs in the corner. He stops to look them over.

"Callaways, baby. I got a set of those.

You play?" Tony asks. "Yes sir."

"I play. What's your handicap?" "About five or six—nothing official."

Tony whistles at the thought of someone that good. "That's pretty good. I've got some buddies that play around here. You could join us sometime."

Grant opens the door to the house and lifts the hand truck stacked with boxes up one step, and pulls it into the house. Tony is right behind him.

Inside, Tony sees that some appliances and furniture have already been delivered and set up.

"Set those boxes in the living room and let's get the fridge set up," Grant instructs Tony.

"Done."

When Tony sets the boxes down in the living room, he notices that there is also furniture there. He thinks nothing of it now, but returns to the kitchen where he helps Grant roll the refrigerator into position and plug it in.

"I've got beer in the basement. You want some?" Grant asks. "I'd love some." "Wait here."

Grant opens a nearby door and descends into the basement. While he waits, Tony stares at the small, bare backyard through the back door.

Soon, Grant returns with two bottles of beer and hands one to Tony. Tony drinks, as does Grant.

"Your backyard looks like it still needs some work," Tony observes.

"Yeah," Grant answers. "I don't know what I want to do with it yet."

Grant opens the back door. Tony follows him into the back yard which turns out to be very shaded, something that Tony couldn't completely tell from inside the house. He squats down and picks up a handful of dirt.

"You'll have trouble growing grass in this," Tony tells Grant.

Tony rises and extends the handful of dirt toward Grant.

"It's too dry," Tony explains. "Look."

Grant tenses imperceptibly, while Tony tosses the dirt away.

"The good side of it is you might not need to mow much," Tony adds.

"Yeah, I'd like to build something back here that would take up lots of space."

"What about a deck?"

"Do you know any carpenters in the area?" Grant asks.

"Construction's my gig," Tony states with clarity. "I'll do it for you. You buy the wood and everything, and I'll build it."

Tony watches Grant stare at the backyard with a concerned expression.

Chapter 2

Petty Annoyances

A few hours later, Tony has returned home. He is in an upstairs bedroom changing into workout clothes while Gigi gathers the sheet, bedspread and pillow cases from the bed. She has asked about Grant.

"As far as I can tell, he's single," Tony says.

"Is he divorced?" Gigi asks.

"I don't know. I'll have to ask next time." "Maybe he's a widower."

"Or he's always been single," Tony offers as an explanation, and then, what he saw there raises doubt in his mind. "Funny thing…he had a lot of furniture already in the house."

"What's funny?" Gigi hasn't caught on to what Tony means.

"Well, he had to really move it all in lickety split by the time I got down there."

Tony sits down on the bed, opens a dresser drawer and pulls out socks that have holes in the heels. He shows the holes to Gigi by sticking his fingers through them. "It didn't seem like the truck was big enough to hold everything he had in that house."

"Maybe he had some of it delivered or brought it in himself before today," Gigi suggests.

"Maybe. I don't know…something doesn't add up, but…I don't know the man."

Once Tony gets his socks and shoes onto his feet, he rises and heads for the hallway.

From there, he descends all the way into the basement.

Tony's basement is essentially, a small gym adorned with boxing posters. Tony has boxing equipment in one corner. When he arrives from upstairs, he puts on gloves and works with a speed bag, slowly at first, gradually getting into a rhythm.

A wall phone rings. Tony ignores it at first and continues to work out, but soon stops and calls out: "GIGI, CAN YOU GET THAT?"

Evidently, Gigi can't hear him. The phone continues to ring. Mildly irritated, Tony picks up the receiver.

"Hello?" he says, and then listens to a voice on the other end of the line. "Yeah, this is the Carson residence." He continues to listen. "Tony Carson. That's me. What did you want?"

Tony listens to silence after that, and then the other party hangs up. It puzzles Tony a little, but, he soon forgets it and goes back to his workout.

After several moments, Tony realizes that tomorrow is trash day. So, he stops and heads upstairs. Trash collection is tomorrow morning.

When Tony gets to the garage, he rolls a full trash receptacle down the driveway toward the curb. Gigi comes around the corner from the backyard.

"You didn't catch that phone call, did you?" Tony asks her.

"I didn't know there was one," she replies.

Tony nods his head casually. He figured that she was somewhere outside and never heard the phone. She goes inside as Tony continues down the driveway.

As Tony nears the curb, Maggie, a 75-year-old woman from next door hurries down her driveway with her trash receptacle, frantic about something.

"You stop stealing my space!" she exclaims.

"I'm not trying to steal your space, Maggie," Tony tries to tell her as calmly as he can.

"I told you before! You stay on your side!" she continues.

This is an encounter that Tony has experienced in the past. He wishes something could be done about his elderly neighbor.

"Maggie, please calm down," Tony pleads.

Maggie arrives at the curb as Tony places his receptacle on the grass between his yard and Maggie's yard.

"Move your damn can!" Maggie is relentless.

"Maggie, I'm on my side. A few inches doesn't make any difference. The trash still gets picked up."

"Move it or I'm calling the cops!" "This is ridiculous," Tony mutters to himself as he moves his receptacle a foot. "That's not far enough! You're still over the line!"

"You just go back in your house and don't worry about it!" Tony is losing his patience.

He regrets raising his voice, but he can't help it.

Inside the house, Gigi is in the kitchen where she can hear the argument outside. Tony's voice gets louder. She heads outside to see if she can end the squabble.

When Gigi is in the driveway, Tony and Maggie are shouting at each other.

"Tony, it's not worth it," Gigi says as she pulls on Tony's arm.

The argument stops, but Tony remains agitated as does Maggie. Grant, dressed in jogging clothes and with what appears to be a bottle of orange Gatorade, strolls by.

"Just let her put the receptacles where she wants," Gigi tells Tony.

"Well, I'm gettin' fed up with it!" Tony says. "Let it be," Gigi says as she pulls Tony toward the house.

"And you stay inside!" Maggie shouts at Tony.

Tony follows Gigi into the house without saying anything further. The incident is over. Maggie isn't well.

The rest of the week is short and easy for Tony. Arrangements for a golf game that includes Grant have been made for Saturday morning. Tony, dressed in a polo shirt and hat, gets his snazzy new SUV out of the garage and heads for Grant's home with his golf clubs in the back. Just as he comes around a bend and turns into Grant's driveway, a tire pops and goes flat. Grant is in his garage waiting.

"Oh no!" he cries out to himself.

Tony manages to get most of his vehicle parked in the driveway enough to not stick out into the street. He gets out and sees the flat tire.

"Just what I need!" he says.

"I wonder what you hit," says Grant. "There isn't time to fix it now," Tony states.

"We'll be late for our tee time."

"I can drive. You get the next one."

Grant helps Tony transfer his golf gear to the back seat of his car, a small sports vehicle with a small back seat. Tony climbs into the passenger seat, and off they go to enjoy a day in the sun on a golf course.

While riding, Tony notices an iron bat on the floor of the back seat.

"You look like you're ready for trouble," Tony begins.

"What?"

"The bat." Tony points at it.

"Oh. Yeah. I have to work in some rough neighborhoods."

"Have you ever used it?"

"Uh-uh," is Grant's reply. "Speaking of neighbors, what was the fuss about with the old lady?"

"Maggie. Oh, she's just a little senile.

She thinks we're trying to steal her garbage can spot. It can get a little crazy with her sometimes."

"How long has she been your neighbor?" Grant asks.

"We've only been here fifteen years and she's been here since. She married money, he died, and she inherited, I hear. She hasn't always been like that."

"Getting old's tough…" Grant says as he turns left at an intersection.

They pass the abandoned shopping center that can be seen through the trees behind their houses.

"It's a shame about that shopping center. My company built it years ago," Tony explains.

"Really? That's interesting. You built it and I'm helping tear it down."

"What do you do?" Tony asks.

"I'm a liquidator. We're clearing it all out." "Yeah, there's lots of places like that these days," Tony says just before he sighs.

Ahead, Stephen and Brian stroll unconcerned in the middle of the street, blocking their path.

"Oh, just what we need," Tony groans.

Grant toots his horn. Stephen and Brian move to the right side of the street. Tony rolls his window down.

"Get your asses out of the street," Tony says to them. "Why aren't you two in school?"

"It's Saturday and it's summer. Why do you think?" Brian retorts.

Slightly embarrassed, Tony rolls up the window. Grant drives on.

The rest of the drive to the golf course is filled with conversation about Tony's past battles with the two boys. But, by the time they arrive, the incident has been dismissed and is no longer relevant.

When they arrive at the golf course, Grant pulls into an open parking space. They get out and unload golf gear.

"We got lots of courses around, but this one's my favorite," Tony tells Grant.

"Do you see your buddies?" Grant asks. Tony looks the parking lot over.

"One of them's car is here. Maybe they rode together."

They gather their clubs and gear bags, and then head for the clubhouse.

"They have a great locker room here," Tony tells Grant matter-of-factly.

The clubs are dropped off at a bag rack outside the pro shop. Then Tony takes Grant to the locker room, where he meets Tony's buddies, Perry, a white man probably in his mid-forties, and Hector, a Latino man in his early fifties, Grant estimates. Both of them have their golf shoes on.

"Heyyy, Perry," Tony exclaims.

The two shake hands. And from there, Tony introduces Grant to his buddies which results in a round of hearty handshakes, jokes and greetings.

Tony and Grant don their golf shoes. After putting their gear in a locker, it's off to the first tee. Tony and Grant arrive there in a golf cart, followed by Hector and Perry. They get out, grab drivers and climb steps to the tee box. Grant puts on two gloves. Tony notices, but says nothing. He's seen people play that way before.

"Ok, what're we doing?" Perry asks the group. "Five dollar Nassau, me and Hector against Tony and Grant?"

"Sounds good to me," Hector says. "I'm in," Tony says, and then turns to Grant. "You cool with that?"

Grant is slow to answer at first. "That's fine."

"Don't worry if it's too much," Tony assures. "I got ya' covered."

All four stretch and loosen up. While this goes on, another foursome ride up to the tee. One of them, a lanky white man with a mustache, has an impatient air about him. It's something that is not perceived yet by Tony, Grant and their foursome.

When their time comes, they tee off, then get in their carts and drive to their shots where they have to wait for the group ahead of them to clear the green. From the 1st tee, a ball lands near them. They look back at the guilty party, the mustached golfer.

"What the hell?" Perry exclaims. "He can see us out here."

"Maybe he ate an extra bowl of Wheaties this morning," Grant kids.

"You know, as long as I've played this game, that happens at least once every year to me," Tony tells the others. "Either someone hits into my group or we're hitting into someone. It's always accidental, though."

"Suuurre," Perry replies with a sarcastic tone. This was no accident.

The group on the green ahead of them finishes, so they are able to finish the hole and head for the second tee.

Just as they did on the first hole, Tony, Grant, Perry and Hector hit their drives into the fairway, but when they again wait for the group ahead to clear the green, a ball from the tee lands among them and bounds forward. They look at each other, then back at the tee.

"What's wrong with that guy?" Tony utters angrily.

After the second hole, they move to the third, a par-3. Grant stands near the flagstick as Perry blasts from a greenside sand trap while Tony and Hector watch. From the tee, the mustached golfer lands a shot on the green. All four men glare at the mustached golfer, before putting out.

As they get into their carts, Tony wheels it around and heads for the tee with Grant alongside. When they get there, he brakes to a squealing halt.

"What the hell's wrong with you hittin' into us that way?!" Tony bellows.

"I'm insured," the man tells them.

"What?!" Tony says, not believing what he just heard.

Grant is dumbfounded too. The other men with the mustached golfer simply stare like they can't do anything to help.

"I've got insurance," the man repeats. "It covers if I hit someone."

"You mean you actually found an insurance company that would sell you liability coverage like that?! " Tony asks.

"Yeah."

"Don't you think we might have some say on whether we like getting hit or not?!" Tony continues to be exasperated by what he's hearing.

"Speed it up some and you wouldn't have that problem."

"I tell you what! If I get hit, I'm coming back here and bust your head open! Does your insurance cover you gettin' hit?!"

"Sounds like a threat to me," the mustached golfer says, and then turns to his buddies. "Don't you think?"

Tony is steamed. He gets out of the cart. Grant gets out and gets between Tony and the man.

"Let me handle this," Grant tells Tony lowly.

Grant turns to the mustached golfer and says: "Sir, have you considered that what you are doing is assault?"

"How?" the man asks.

"It's assault-with-a-deadly-weapon. A golf ball can kill you if it hits you right. Did you consider that?"

The mustached golfer realizes now.

"So, I'll tell you this only once. If one more golf ball from you lands in our foursome, we're going to call the law and have you arrested.

Got it?"

The mustached golfer stares back blankly. "Let's go," Grant says to Tony.

They get back in their cart and head back toward the third green where Hector and Perry wait. Tony drives slowly at first.

"Can you believe that idiot?" Grant queries.

"Thanks for stepping in," Tony says to him. "I've got kind of a bad temper sometimes."

"I hate fighting in the morning before I've had a couple beers," Grant says.

Grant picks up a cup filled with a beverage. As he tips it to drink, Tony accelerates. Grant spills the beverage down the front of his shirt.

Chapter 3

Troubling Revelations

The rest of the round turns into a pleasant day for Tony, Grant and their two buddies.

Tony goes home satisfied with a pretty good day. Later that night, Gigi is in bed clothes, as is Tony who is in the bathroom brushing his teeth. Gigi draws the covers back on the bed.

"You were lucky Grant was there," Gigi says. "You might've ended up in jail."

"Yeah, I don't want to do that again," Tony answers from the bathroom sink.

Tony finishes up and crosses to the bed. "Besides, you're too old to be getting into fights. What if you lost?" Gigi points out. "Who? Me? Never."

"You never know."

Tony sits on the bed and says: "Yeah, well. Grant seems like a good guy, though. Tough golfer."

"What did he shoot?"

"Seventy something…he's kind of quiet.

Too quiet almost."

Tony turns off the light and gets under the covers.

Later that night when Tony and Gigi are asleep, there is a loud click at the window, followed quickly by another click on the opposite wall. They sleep undisturbed.

When morning comes, Tony is up and alert, ready for the day. He gets into his street clothes before a mirror while Gigi lingers in bed. She rolls over to look out the bedroom window and she sees a tiny hole in the glass.

"Honey, what is that?" she asks. Tony turns to her.

"What?"

Gigi points at the hole.

"Something in the window?" he asks as he goes to the window and examines the hole. "I think it looks like a bullet hole."

Unsure what to do next, Tony goes to the phone and makes a call to the police. Within ten minutes, someone rings the front door bell. When Tony opens it, he is greeted by a police officer, a white man, whose last name is Miller. Officer Miller is all that Tony remembers. He takes Officer Miller to the master bedroom where Tony and Gigi watch him examine the hole in the glass.

"You're right, it's a bullet hole," Officer Miller says.

Tony and Gigi stares at the hole very concerned.

Officer Miller goes to the wall opposite the hole in the glass, on the other side of the bed and finds a chipped hole in the wall.

"Here's the bullet," Officer Miller continues as he digs the bullet out with a pocket knife. "It's a .22. It's low caliber but, the hole it makes is enough to kill you."

"Bobby Kennedy was killed with a .22," Tony observes.

"It's a popular caliber for assassins," Officer Miller says.

"Somebody was shooting at us?!" Gigi exclaims.

"We haven't established that yet," Officer Miller tells her.

The issue with the bullet in the wall of the bedroom doesn't end with Tony. A few days later, he is at Grant's house to help build the deck in his back yard that he promised. Tony and Grant wait next to a truck loaded with the equipment they need, both wearing thick work gloves.

"You were damn lucky one of you wasn't up walking around when that bullet came in the window," Grant tells Tony after hearing about the incident.

"Even if we were and it missed, we would have both panicked," Tony says. "Whoever it was picked a great time. We were asleep."

"You don't think it was intentional, do you?"

"What other reason would there be?" Tony queries. "Unless they were just trying to scare us."

"Well, stray bullets wind up in all kinds of strange places. When people shoot guns into the air, the bullet has to come down somewhere."

"Yeah, but, this shot was level. It wasn't traveling downward. The hole in the wall was level with the hole in the glass."

Tony shrugs his shoulders. "It still could've been a stray."

Two cars arrive and park next to the curb in the street. Perry and Hector get out, dressed to get dirty.

"Alright," Tony exclaims with enthusiasm. "Recruits have arrived."

Tony lowers the back of the truck with the deck material. It's all unloaded and taken to the backyard.

Construction of the deck begins. Perry and Hector dig holes with post-hole diggers while Tony examines a blueprint. Grant watches, seemingly uncertain on how to help.

"Grant, you know what all this means, don't you?" Perry asks. "You're going to invite us all over for a party free of charge when this is all done."

"Yeah, and you supply the beer," Tony adds.

"How can I help?" Grant asks them. "Get the wheelbarrow out of the truck,"

Tony says.

Grant heads around the house. A moment later, he returns, frantic. The work gloves are off as he runs for the back door and enters the house.

"Did he cut himself?" Hector asks, concerned, as are all three men.

"I didn't see any blood," Perry says.

Tony follows after Grant to see what the problem is. Inside, the house, he looks around to get his bearings. He's only been in here once. When he spots the hallway, he follows it to the bathroom where Grant scrubs his hands furiously with soap and water. Tony leans in.

"Are you okay?" Tony asks. "I will be."

"What happened?"

"The gloves were knocked off," Grant explains. "Dirt got on my hands."

"You got one of those obsessive-compulsive disorders, huh?"

"You're the first person I've known to recognize it right off the bat," Grant says. "Have you told a doctor?" Tony asks. "Yeah, but there's nothing that can be done. I can't help it."

"Hm, that's too bad," Tony states. "I think you can help it… " Tony cuts off what he is about to say. It's not proper right now. "Okay, come on out and help when you can."

Chapter 4

Disturbing Discoveries

On the following Saturday evening after a round of golf with his buddies, Tony has a grill fired up in his backyard with meat cooking and beverages in coolers. His deck is under the shadow of the house. There is also a newly-built artificial putting green. Tony is at the corner of the house hosing off digging tools as Gigi, Perry and Hector exit from his house through a glass sliding door with beers. They take a seat in folding lawn chairs.

"You better hurry up while the beer's still cold, Tony," Perry says.

"In a minute," Tony tells him.

"So, do we head down to Grant's house for party time next week?" Gigi asks.

"If you want to show up and no one's there, you can," Perry replies.

"The deck's ready, but Grant's not," Tony explains. "His job doesn't allow him much time, right now."

"He'll get around to it," says Hector.

Just then, Tony sees Grant pass by the front yard in his jogging clothes and carrying his bottle of orange Gatorade.

"He just walked by," Tony tells the others. "I thought he was out of town."

"Why didn't he stop?" Gigi asks.

Tony shrugs his shoulders as he finishes and takes the tools around to the front of the house, then returns and joins the others.

In the woods behind the house, Maggie picks blackberries and puts them into a bag. Perry has been watching her closely.

"You know what? I bet she makes great pies," he observes."

Tony drinks down a bottle of beer, then starts another.

The conversation starts to wane, so Hector tries to stir things up with something all are interested in.

"The Dow's up. Did you see?" he asks Perry.

"Yeah. That's great. It's probably the only time when lots of bull is welcome," Perry replies, then snickers.

"It never made sense to me what a farm animal has to do with economics. A bull and a bear?" Gigi queries.

"If you can tell the difference between chickenshit and chicken salad, it's not hard," Tony answers.

Gigi shakes her head, puzzled. The remark makes no sense, but she realizes that it might be the alcohol.

"It's a fine line…" Hector adds. "Speaking of lines," Tony says as he opens a third beer and eyes Maggie in the woods. His speech is now slurred. "HEY MAGGIE! YOU BETTER STAY ON YOUR SIDE OF THE LINE!"

Maggie hears his voice, but doesn't comprehend what he said. She simply stares, and then goes back to picking blackberries.

"What are you doing?" Perry asks him, now a little embarrassed by his behavior.

"She's closer to our house than hers," he answers.

Perry and Hector look at him sardonically as they finish their beers.

"I tell you what," Perry announces. "I'm going to call it a day."

"Me too," Hector says.

They both get to their feet, not wanting to contend with Tony in his alcoholic stupor.

"Thanks for the beer, Gigi," Perry says. "Tony, I'll see you again when you're sober."

"Me too," Hector adds.

Perry and Hector say nothing more as they hurry to leave.

"Time for bed, don't you think?" Gigi suggests to Tony.

"I want to stay out here for awhile," Tony tells her.

Gigi enters the house. This isn't the usual time they go to bed. Instead of arguing, she leaves Tony alone. He continues to stare at Maggie.

"On your side, Maggie," he says loudly without shouting.

"You leave me alone!" Maggie utters. "Yeah, yeah," Tony mutters.

Tony relaxes, and soon falls asleep. A series of small explosions startle Tony awake. As he looks around, Stephen and Brian laugh as they cross from the woods through Tony's yard toward the street.

"You mothers!" Tony growls at them. "It wasn't us," Brian says.

"You expect me to believe that?" Tony challenges.

"The firecrackers were already there when we started across," Brian continues.

"I thought I told you two to stay off my property!" Tony bellows.

"So, have us arrested," Stephen says to Tony.

The boys laugh derisively as they disappear around the corner.

Tony hurries after them, determined to put a stop to their defiance. But, when he turns the corner, the boys are gone.

The following morning, having dismissed the firecrackers as a prank by the two boys, even though they said that they had nothing to do with it, Tony is still mad. He leaves the house through the garage, cranky and mumbling to himself.

"Damn people shootin' fireworks when it ain't even the Fourth Of July. I need my sleep. A man can't function with no damn sleep. I can't."

When he gets to the driveway, the front door opens and Gigi is there.

"Tony, have you seen the newspaper?" she asks.

Tony turns toward her. "The newspaper?

Since when did you start reading the newspaper?"

"Ever since I moved to this country." "You don't need no newspaper."

"You're right. I can always rely on you to tell me everything you know. It takes about two seconds." Gigi is fed up with Tony's attitude.

Tony glares at her.

"You straighten up and find it for me," she orders. "I got my sleep last night."

Tony calms down and looks toward his SUV. He sees the newspaper underneath.

"It's under the damn truck."

Tony gets on his stomach and tries to reach it.

"I can't get it," he groans.

"Why don't you move the truck?" It's a simple solution to Gigi.

Tony, still on his stomach, stretches and grabs the newspaper.

"What's wrong with the lawn?" Tony hears Gigi ask.

"What?"

"The lawn," she says. "It's brown."

Tony gets to his feet and sees dead brown spots all over the lawn.

"Oh no! What in the hell happened?!" Tony walks out onto the lawn to look closer.

"You put too much fertilizer on it," Gigi suggests.

"No!" Tony replies. "I've never used too much fertilizer as long as we've lived here! It's measured to exact specs every time!"

Tony says nothing for several moments while he stares at the grass. He bends down to look at a brown spot closely.

"I think someone's done something to it," Tony utters without hesitation.

Gigi joins him on the lawn. She bends down and sniffs the grass.

"It smells like gasoline," she says.

The gasoline-drenched grass dies. It irritates Tony, but the only recourse is to replace it. When Grant learns about it, he allows Tony to bring his vehicle and load sod from a stack next to the side of his house.

"I sure do thank you for this, Grant," Tony says as he and Gigi carry strips of sod.

"Oh, no problem,"Grant replies. "Thanks for helping me build that deck."

"I'll pay you as soon as I can," Tony tells him. "I'll pay you double what you paid."

"I can't imagine why someone would pour gasoline on your grass," Grant speculates. "I mean, why?"

"Oh, there's probably a dozen people who would have reason," Gigi points out.

Tony stops and glares at her: "Oh, come on. It's not that bad."

He then turns to Grant to explain further: "I've gotten into it with people in the area."

"Like that screwball at the golf course?" Grant inquires. "That doesn't sound very conducive for 'neighbors sticking together.' Have you ever thought of trying out anger management classes?"

"I've been telling him that for years," Gigi says.

"Nah, I'm only dangerous when I want to be," Tony explains as he loads the last strip of grass. "Didn't you use to get into fights when you were a kid?"

"No, not really," answers Grant.

"Tony thinks that all boys get into fights," Gigi tells Grant. "I keep telling him it isn't so."

"She's right," says Grant. "It's a sickness actually."

Tony opens the driver's side door on his SUV thinking deeply before he climbs in. Just then, a smoke alarm goes off in Maggie's house next door.

Tony and Grant rush to the house while Gigi makes a 911 call. There doesn't seem to be a fire, which leads Tony and Grant to determine that there is no dire emergency, but they stand by in case they're needed until a firetruck arrives, in addition to Officer Miller in a police car.

He goes into the house with the firemen. Soon after, he leaves and heads toward them in Tony's driveway.

"Thanks for calling us, folks," Officer Miller begins.

"What's up?" Tony asks him.

"She forgot to turn off a burner on her stove," Officer Miller explains.

"We all do that sometimes," says Grant. "Yes, but she's been doing it a lot lately,"

Officer Miller says further. "This is the first time a fire started."

Chapter 5

Papa Bear And His Cub

After much preparation and delay, Grant's deck is finally ready. It is a Saturday evening when he invites his new friends over for a celebration. Hector and Perry, with their wives, are the first ones to arrive.

Grant has a grill set up, a cooler of beer in one corner and food on a table as tango music plays, something that is very foreign to the ears of everyone in attendance.

Tony and Gigi round the corner of the house carrying a covered dish. With them is a young, pretty, black girl. Grant immediately is attracted to her. He estimates that she is about twenty and he can't keep his eyes off of her.

"Welcome, welcome, welcome," Grant says to them.

"Grant, I want you to meet Rhea, my daughter," Tony says to him.

"Your daughter?" Grant asks, and then shakes her hand gently. "A pretty girl.

Welcome."

Rhea's bashful smile is one that will light up a room.

"Thank you," she says softly.

"Please, sit and grab a bite to eat," Grant tells Tony's family.

As Tony quickly gets a plate of food and sits, Grant leans on the rail near Tony as he watches Rhea.

"It's funny," Grant begins. "I never thought of you having kids."

"She's my one and only," Tony replies. "My pride and joy."

"I thought your lawn was your pride and joy."

"That's my second pride and joy. My third, actually. My daughter is my number one and my marriage is my second."

"Ah, that makes sense," Grant states with a chuckle. "Your daughter's a college kid, I presume?"

"Yeah. She's home visitin' for awhile." Rhea and Gigi finally have plates of food.

They sit nearby.

"What's that weird music you got playin'?" Tony asks Grant.

"I'm glad you like it," Grant says sarcastically.

"You have to excuse Tony," Perry explains. "The man has no couth."

"It's tango," Grant explains.

"Why the hell are you playin' that?" Tony asks after a guffaw.

Grant shrugs his shoulders. "Because I like it. I'm into ballroom."

Rhea hasn't been listening to the conversation that closely until that comment.

"Oooh. I've always wanted to learn. Are you any good?" Rhea asks.

"Pretty good," Grant tells her. "Started in high school."

"I never was into crap like that," Tony says.

"Ballroom is music of the ages," Grant explains. "It's never a fad. Didn't you want to find ways to attract girls when you were a teenager?"

"Wasn't much into fads either," Tony states further. "Wasn't into girls much. I was into fightin' and boxin'. I was a wild child."

Grant winces subtly before adding: "Oh, come now. What about the words that were popular back then? 'Groovy.' Remember that?"

"Yeah, I remember. We used to say, 'right on' and 'let's get it on'. You're right. Those were fads," Tony says, and then laughs.

"Cool's still used," Rhea says to them. "Those other phrases I hear when I listen to old Marvin Gaye songs on the radio."

"Yeah, he was a helluva singer," says Tony with a big smile. "Wonder what happened to him?"

"Oh, c'mon, Tony," Perry says. "He's dead. His father went nuts and shot him."

"Oh, that's right," Tony answers. "It still was a great time back then. The good old days."

After dinner, the evening slows down into one of casual conversation and dancing. The dancing eventually becomes everyone else watching Tony teach tango to Rhea.

In Grant's kitchen, Tony and Gigi wash dishes in the sink where they can watch the others through a window.

"I came to the party to get away from washing dishes," Gigi exclaims.

"It doesn't hurt to pitch in and help," Tony points out. "Grant really put out for us."

On the deck, they watch Grant lead Rhea through basic tango steps; promenade, then outside and inside fans.

"They're getting a little close, don't you think?" Tony asks Gigi.

"Ballroom's all about love and lust. Calm down," Gigi explains.

"I'm calm," Tony adds. "I just don't know if I like a man touching my daughter like that."

"She's letting him."

Soon, the dance is over. Grant and Rhea come inside. Rhea has a look of excitement in her eyes.

"Daddy, Grant has agreed to teach me to dance," Rhea announces.

"If that's alright with you two," Grant adds. "I guess it's okay," Tony says. "Where are you going to teach?"

"Here," replies Grant. "I'm building a studio in my basement. You and Gigi should come down with Rhea and learn."

"I don't think so…a big gorilla like me?" Tony is embarrassed by the suggestion.

"The last time we danced close, he nearly broke my toes," Gigi explains.

Grant laughs and pats Tony on the shoulder.

The party continues on into the night. Soft music plays. Everyone is up dancing slow, including Tony and Gigi. Grant dances with Rhea at a polite distance. The mood is very romantic.

When the party ends, almost at midnight, Tony, Gigi and Rhea make the short drive home. Tony takes it slow in order to reflect on the evening.

"That was one of the best parties I've ever been to," Tony announces.

"Grant thinks I could be very good at ballroom with some practice," Rhea says from the back seat.

"You were looking good out there," Gigi tells her.

"There's a ballroom team at school," Rhea says. "I'm going to sign up for it next fall."

Grant has made an impression on Rhea. "The paths our lives follow," Tony comments.

There is silence for a few moments, and then Rhea has a question: "Daddy, what did you mean about fighting and boxing? You never talked much about when you were young."

"Oh, I was kind of a bad kid. I used to get into a lot of fights…settled every problem with my fists. That's why I got into boxing. I liked to fight."

"It sounds awful violent," Rhea says. "It's not something I'm very proud of. I guess that's why

I never talked about it much." "And you stopped boxing before I was born, right?" Rhea suggests.

"I made him stop," Gigi exclaims.

"We thought it was best for you," Tony explains. "I did pretty good as a pro, but wasn't making enough to support a family." "He used to come home with his face all beat up and bruised," Gigi states. "Sometimes one of his eyes would be swollen shut."

"Sometimes both," says Tony. "I see…" Rhea says softly.

They arrive home and pull into the driveway. Tony's SUV is there and an old used car parked on the curb.

"Daddy, I'm glad you gave up fighting," Rhea announces.

In the headlights, new patches of sod on the lawn can be seen.

"I'm going to pulverize whoever did that when I find them," Tony utters menacingly.

Tony taps a button on a remote and the garage doors open.

Rhea laughs. "No one says pulverize anymore."

Tony steers into the garage. The garage doors close behind them.

The following morning is another bright sunny day. The front door opens at Tony's house, and Rhea steps out dressed in jogging clothes. She proceeds down the driveway to the sidewalk where she goes through a series of stretches.

Inside the front window, Tony watches her as he casually sips from a cup of coffee. He sees her jog down the sidewalk toward a bend in the street.

Coming from the opposite direction is a snazzy red Jeep. Tony sees Brian driving with Stephen in the passenger seat. He also sees them ogle Rhea as they follow her. Tony tears for the door.

In the driveway, Tony starts the engine to his vehicle, backs out into the street, and speeds toward the last spot where he saw the Jeep.

Tony drives around the bend, glancing down winding side streets. Rhea is nowhere in sight, but he sees the Jeep far ahead. Tony steps on the gas. He catches up with the Jeep, speeds around until he is parallel with it and forces the boys to the curb.

Tony gets out and rushes to the Jeep.

Brian rolls down the window.

"What the hell are you doing?" Brian asks angrily.

"Where is she?!" Tony demands. "Who?"

"My daughter!" Tony glances into the back seat. It's empty, as far as he can tell, but he can't see all of it. "I need to see in your back seat!"

"Are you off your meds or somethin'?!" Brian asks.

"OPEN THE DOOR!" Tony screams. "Alright, alright." Brian rolls the back seat window down. Tony sees no one else in the vehicle.

"What did you do with her?!" Tony continues his rage.

"Hey, man, calm down."

Stephen leans over from the passenger seat. "Tell us who you're talking about.

Maybe we can help."

"My daughter! You were following her!" "The cute chick?" Stephen asks. "That was your daughter?"

Stephen smirks as he whistles lowly, then thumps the seat with his hand.

"IF YOU TOUCHED HER, I'M GOING TO BREAK YOU IN HALF!"

Stephen and Brian snicker at Tony's angst.

"Hey, she's with the new dude," Brian tells Tony. "They went down one of these streets."

Tony rushes back to his vehicle and gets in without saying anything further to the two boys. With the engine still running, he drives away, calmer than a little while ago, but still in a lather. He gets a cell phone out, pushes buttons and puts it to his ear.

"Gigi, I can't find Rhea," he says into the phone when Gigi answers, and then listens. "She's there?"

Tony hasn't calmed down entirely yet. He is still suspicious as he pulls away in his vehicle. He isn't sorry about his behavior toward the two boys. They still might be behind something no good, Tony thinks to himself.

When Tony arrives back home, he enters the kitchen through the garage to find Rhea and Gigi there.

"Where have you been?" he asks Rhea. "Out jogging," Rhea replies.

"Who were you with?"

"Grant," Rhea explains. "Calm down.

Nothing happened."

"They ran into each other and decided to jog together," Gigi says.

Tony starts to relax now. "I saw those two boys follow you. I thought they were going to bother you."

"They were bothering me," Rhea says. "But, Grant came along and chased them away."

"He's outside," Gigi tells Tony.

Tony has mixed feelings. One is that he is still suspicious about Grant's intentions, but he also feels a sense of relief that nothing happened to his daughter.

He goes to the back door where he sees Grant practicing on the putting green. Tony opens the door and climbs down the steps of his deck with a big smile on his face. Grant sees him.

"I'll never be able to thank you enough," Tony tells Grant.

"For what?" Grant asks, unaware of how worried Tony was.

"For my daughter...I saw those boys follow her."

"She's got a good head on her shoulders, Tony. You have nothing to worry about."

"I just got excited." Tony is self-analyzing. "I assumed and that led to assuming something else and..."

"Well, wouldn't there be less to worry about if she jogged with someone?" Grant suggests.

"Yeah. You're right."

"I'm going to have to install one of these in my backyard," Grant says as he sinks a putt. "This is nice."

42

Chapter 6

Escalation

A day or two later, days that are without further incident, Tony, Gigi and Rhea are together at the dinner table enjoying a fabulous meal. Rhea eats faster than her parents, thus, she is nearly finished with her plate.

"This is good," Tony comments casually to Gigi. "What is it, chicken?" he asks as he pokes the meat to examine it.

"Pheasant," Gigi answers. "Pheasant? Where'd you find that?" "Down at the Asian store. Chinese." "Why would a Chinese store have pheasant?" Tony inquires. "I thought they only sold Chinese cuisine."

"Rhea laughs as she explains: "Oh, daddy. You're so funny. Pheasant is native to China."

"Don't laugh at your dear old dad like that," Tony replies, kidding with her. "College girl. What class did you learn that in?"

"I learned that back in high school," Rhea states.

"Well, it's still good," says Tony. "The green onion and sauce…mmmm-mmm."

There is silence for a few moments as Rhea wolfs down her meal.

"I'll be gone for a few hours, just so you know," Rhea tells them.

"Where are you going?" Gigi asks. "Grant's. My first dance lesson is tonight,"

Rhea says as she gets up and takes her empty plate and used silverware to the sink.

"Are you going now?" Tony asks. "Yes."

"Have fun," Gigi tells her.

When Rhea goes to the living room, Tony becomes concerned.

"She's going by herself?" he asks Gigi. "It's just down the street," Gigi explains. "There's still plenty of light."

Still not satisfied, Tony gets up and heads for the living room where he sees Rhea open the front door.

"Call when it's time to come…" Tony says to her.

Rhea, getting tired of her father's worrying, leaves and closes the door behind her without saying anything further.

Tony, unsure whether his daughter heard him or was just ignoring him, tells Gigi that he is going to for a walk, intending on following Rhea. Gigi quietly understands.

Outside, Tony walks slowly down the sidewalk in the direction of Grant's home.

When he arrives, he quietly follows the driveway to the side of the house. Softly, he hears the Pink Panther Theme coming from the basement.

In Grant's basement, wood paneled walls and a wood dance floor dominate one end, in addition to two benches that line one wall.

Grant holds Rhea in classic ballroom position as they advance around the dance floor, doing foxtrot. The music plays from a stereo system.

"Slow, slow, quick, quick," Grant says, and they stop. "Again. Slow, slow, quick, quick."

Rhea improves each time, but Grant wants her to stop and absorb what she has learned before progressing further.

"Very good," he tells her. "Let's take a break."

Grant stops the music as they sit. A light in the corner of the ceiling blinks.

"What's that?" Rhea asks.

"I have a motion detector on the side of the house," Grant explains. "Somebody's out there. Wait here."

Grant goes upstairs as Rhea waits with a touch of apprehension.

Outside, Tony crosses Odysseus Drive and hides behind a tree. Grant opens the front door, looks around, then goes back inside.

When Grant returns to the basement, Rhea is drinking water from a cooler.

"Your father's across the street hiding behind a tree," Grant tells her.

Rhea chuckles.

"Should I invite him in?" Grant asks. "No. He'll just be embarrassed." "He's checking up on you."

"I know." Rhea is more interested in learning to dance than what her father is doing. "Now, where can I find foxtrot music to practice on?"

"Easy. Just get any good Frank Sinatra CD. The man was the foxtrot king."

"Really?"

"Let's work on some steps." Grant turns on some different music as they get up.

Two or three hours go by before Rhea's dance lesson is over and she leaves with Grant by her side. Tony, still under the tree, watches Grant escort Rhea around the bend and disappear. His legs hurt from standing in one spot too long. He waits several moments as Grant returns and enters his house.

Tony heads down the sidewalk toward his house. Brian and Stephen, in the Jeep, cruise slowly past his house, then past him. When they notice him, they keep going.

Tony waits across from his house, studying the neighborhood.

The garage door on Maggie's house opens and Maggie rolls her trash receptacle to the curb. She sees Tony.

"I see you over there sneakin' around," she says loudly.

"Don't be so sure, Maggie," Tony answers back. "I'm not as crooked as I'm supposed to be."

"You just wait right there."

Maggie scurries back inside her house. Tony smirks at her. Maggie returns with a camera and snaps his picture. The flash blinds Tony.

"Now, whatever you're up to, I have proof you were out here," Maggie cries out. "You just wait."

"I can't get far now. You got me." Tony refuses to take this encounter seriously. "Tar and feathers wouldn't be good enough for you," Maggie says. "You just wait." "Tar and feathers? Sounds pretty kinky to me." Tony has to laugh at that one.

Maggie didn't expect a reply like that. Her voice is softer: "You just wait." She scurries into her garage. The door goes down.

Tony crosses the street and enters his house, smug about his ability to deal with Maggie. Humor. That's it.

When Tony is in, he hears voices in the kitchen. There, Rhea helps Gigi load dishes into a dishwasher. Tony gets a beer out of the refrigerator and opens it.

"Were you looking out for me, daddy?" Rhea asks him.

"What do you mean?" Tony asks as he drinks the beer.

"We saw you out there behind that tree," she explains.

"Oh, well…"

Rhea sees that her father is embarrassed. "You're so silly sometimes, but I'm glad you are," Rhea teases.

Tony and Rhea smile at each other. Rhea goes to him and kisses him on the cheek.

From outside, there is a violent explosion, something that none of them have heard before in their lives. All three jump and take several moments to calm down enough to determine where it came from.

When they go to the living room to see what happened, Tony sees through the front window that his SUV is engulfed in flames. They all go outside.

"Oh no!" he cries out. "What happened?
Call 911!"

Tony goes to the garage and opens it. "Rhea, help me!" he utters in a frightened voice.

Tony and Rhea roll out a garden hose, hook it to a faucet and dowse the fire.

Chapter 7

Fireworks

Once again, a fire truck and a police car are outside Tony's house. So are neighbors, including Maggie, all there to see what the excitement is. The fire has been extinguished, but the question of who did this remains.

"Retribution has been served, Tony Carson!" Maggie calls out. "What goes around, comes around!"

Tony and his family can only glare at her.

She isn't funny this time. As this goes on, Officer Miller approaches Tony.

"We poked around and it appears that someone threw a cherry bomb under your truck," he informs Tony. "The gas tank was ruptured by the explosion and caused the fire."

"A bomb?!" Gigi exclaims in horror.

Disgusted, Tony puts his hands on his hips. Gigi and Rhea are aghast.

Tony's latest round of roller coaster events continues into a more peaceful interlude after he files a claim to replace his SUV. But, the incident is still on his mind when he joins in a round of golf on the following weekend. Tony, Grant, Perry and Hector wait in carts for a group ahead of them to tee off.

"It doesn't make sense," Tony tells his buddies after explaining what happened. "What's the point of destroying my ride?"

"I would speculate that the perpetrators got more than they intended," Perry opines.

"You mean they got lucky?" Tony asks. "You were the main target, not the truck,"

Grant says, suggesting another way to look at it.

"It has to be those kids," Hector suggests. "Yeah, but how do I prove it?" Tony speculates.

"They were bothering your daughter, by the way," Grant says. "I normally like to jog alone, but she needed help."

"Hey, I'm glad you did, buddy," says Tony. "Tony here's like a big papa bear with his kid," Perry kids. "Mess with her and he'll take your head off."

"Wouldn't you be?" Tony gripes. He doesn't always care for certain kinds of teasing.

"I think you need to back off and give her some room to breathe," Perry tells him.

"Hey, you mind your own damn business!" Tony is getting steamed.

"Calm down," Grant says.

Tony is silent for a moment or two as he gathers his thoughts.

"It doesn't sound like you have many options with those boys," Hector points out. "You have to catch them in the act, which isn't easy."

"I think we need to start a block watch," Tony says.

"Yeah, but, you're the only one having a problem," Hector states.

"It might not be the boys," Grant posits. The group ahead of them clears the tee.

It's now their turn to tee off. The mustached golfer that Tony blew up at for hitting shots into them is among that group. There is an uncomfortable moment as he and Tony stare at each other. Tony is becoming a little suspicious.

Tony and Grant's foursome plays behind the mustached golfer all day. And all day, he glares at Tony every time they're within eye shot of each other. On the back nine, Tony finally mentions something to Grant.

"That dude has been giving me the evil eye all day today. I wonder if it's him."

"I think he's always like that," says Grant. "No, it's someone else around here."

"I wish I could figure it out."

Tony rode with Grant on this trip, the idea being that they would trade driving, but being that Tony is temporarily without a vehicle, Grant has volunteered to do all of it until Tony gets a replacement. There is a second, older car at home, but, Tony doesn't like to leave Gigi stranded with no transportation.

The drive home from the golf course is filled with trivial conversation about golf, until they arrive at Tony's home. Grant pulls into his driveway. He punches a button that causes the trunk to pop open. They get out.

Tony gets his golf clubs and a gear bag out, then nods toward Maggie's house: "Next door," he suggests. "Do you think she's capable of it?"

"It's possible," Grant agrees. "Something else to consider. You might not even be the target. Maybe whoever did it got the wrong house."

"I don't know about that," says Tony. "Well, anyways, you played good today." Grant and Tony shake hands. "I might be out of town next weekend. I'll give you a call."

"Yeah. Okay," Tony says as he heads for the garage. Grant gets in his car, backs out and drives toward home.

Maggie rounds the corner of her house, wandering aimlessly toward her mailbox near the curb, seemingly lost. Tony watches her. Maggie goes to her mailbox and stares at it for several seconds, in a quandary.

"Maggie, is something wrong?" Tony asks. Maggie stares at him, but doesn't answer,

as if she doesn't recognize him. Finally, she heads for her front door and enters her house.

Tony opens his garage door and puts his golf clubs away, now concerned for his neighbor. That's not the same woman he's had to contend with for so many years.

When he enters the house and goes into the kitchen, Gigi and Rhea sit at a table with a stack of magazines and business reply envelopes in front of them.

"What's with the magazines?" Tony asks, puzzled, and very suspicious considering what has been happening to him the past few weeks.

"We don't know," Gigi tells him.

"They were all in the mailbox today," Rhea says.

"What are you doing?" Tony asks.

"We're filling out these little cards with the invoices telling them we didn't order these," says Gigi.

"Most of them are women's fashion and stuff like that. We know you didn't order them and we certainly didn't…" Rhea adds.

"What is going on?!" Tony inquires to no one. "Is someone trying to ruin my credit or something?!"

"Oh, it wouldn't do that," Rhea states firmly. "It's just a mistake. Your name made it on some mailing list somewhere."

"Like I have time to read all these magazines and then unsubscribe to every one of them," Tony moans. "Somebody's really getting under my skin."

"Help us get these cards filled out," Gigi tells him.

Tony sighs as he sits down and helps.

On the morning of July 4th, Tony is standing in his living room impatiently staring out the front window. A sprinkler turns on outside, obscuring his view of the street. Gigi enters from the kitchen stirring a bowl of potato salad.

"What are you waiting for?" Gigi asks Tony.

"It's a surprise," Tony replies. "For who, me or Rhea?"

"Mostly for Rhea, but I wanted to surprise you too."

"Just when I don't need surprises, you come up with one. I need help getting the food ready for this afternoon." Gigi is preparing for an all-day community picnic that takes place in a park that is a just few miles away. It's a lot of work, but the camaraderie that occurs makes the event worth the effort.

"I was guaranteed it would be here this morning." Tony is ignoring Gigi's plight.

Cooking isn't his thing. "What's going to be here?"

"I'm not going to tell you," Tony says with a smirk. "You have to wait and see."

"Do you want me to wake Rhea?" "No. Wait 'til it arrives."

Gigi turns to head back to the kitchen. "Here they are." Tony can barely contain his excitement.

Tony goes to the door, nearly opens it, but then starts up the stairs, confused about what to do first. He comes back down the stairs to the door, then decides to get Rhea first.

"Rhea? Wake up," Tony shouts, and then opens the front door. "I'll be right out," he speaks loudly to people outside. He goes upstairs.

When Tony enters Rhea's bedroom, Rhea is in bed not very awake, her eyes still closed.

"Rhea?" Tony calls out softly. Rhea opens her eyes.

"I got something for you downstairs, baby," Tony says.

"What is it?" she asks. "You have to come see."

"I want to sleep some more," Rhea replies in a squeaky voice.

"Okay, if you don't want it, I'll just have the men take it away."

Rhea's curiosity is piqued. She wakens very quickly.

"You need to get up for this one."

That does it. Rhea realizes that it's worth getting out of bed. When she gets up to dress, Tony leaves and closes the door behind him.

When everyone is up and dressed in street clothes, they step outside to find that a new car is parked in the driveway, and the old used car is on a trailer, ready to be taken away. Rhea's jaw drops. In addition is a new SUV, Tony's replacement vehicle.

"Is that for me?" Rhea asks. "Yessirree," Tony tells her. "All yours."

Rhea is super happy. She jumps up and down after hugging and kissing Tony.

"That old car was turning into a clunker," Tony announces. "I decided it was time for a change."

Gigi circles the new car, looking it over. "It's beautiful. How'd you do it?" she asks. Tony shrugs as he gets the keys from a man by the trailer and hands them to Rhea. "Thanks, man," he tells the driver.

"Can I take it out for a spin?" Rhea asks. "Sure. It's insured, gassed up and ready to go," Tony informs her.

Rhea climbs in and starts the engine. She backs out of the driveway and waves to her parents with a giant grin as she drives away.

It doesn't take long before she is on the freeway breezing along to see how fast the car can go.

Back home, Tony loads picnic paraphernalia into his vehicle. The front door opens and Gigi approaches him to tell him that Rhea called.

"She said to go ahead without her and she'd find us at the park," she informs Tony.

The drive to the park takes all of five minutes. Lots of people are there busily setting up blankets and picnic areas. Tony and Gigi carry their things across grass to two picnic tables where Perry and Hector are with their wives.

"Heeyyy, have you got the grill fired up?" Tony calls out to them.

"Not yet," Perry says. "Thought we'd wait for you. That's your specialty."

A mile or two outside of town, Rhea pulls into the parking lot of a McDonald's where she parks next to Grant's car. She gets out and casually enters the restaurant where she sees Grant wave at her from a booth.

Rhea orders food and joins Grant at the booth.

"Thanks for coming," says Grant. "I get tired of eating alone so much."

"Oh, you're welcome," Rhea answers. "How do you like my new car?" She bites into a burger as she asks this.

"It's a beauty. Did your dad buy that?" "Yeah."

"How'd he swing it?"

"It had something to do with when the truck was destroyed. His company was going to get rid of it anyway, so he used the insurance money to buy the car too."

"Must be nice."

"You sound jealous," Rhea tells him as she looks into his eyes.

"I am a little. I wish I could do things like that. It looks like he doesn't have to do much. The company kind of runs itself."

"It does. He just has to go in a couple times a week. I don't know who blew up daddy's car, but, it turned out to be a good thing."

"He wasn't mad?" Grant asks.

"Oh, he always gets mad when bad things happen, but daddy can fix just about anything."

At the park, Grant has the grill going with several kinds of meat cooking. He watches as Gigi joins other families in a game of horseshoes. A community coming together that he sees take place at this event every year makes him feel good inside. He wishes that Rhea would hurry up and join them.

Inside the McDonald's restaurant, Rhea and Grant are still seated at the same booth. Grant glances around nervously.

"What's wrong?" Rhea asks him. Rhea has been casually eating an order of french fries, but stops when she sees that something is bothering him.

"Nothing," he replies.

"Why are you glancing around?" "It's just something I never got over." "What do you mean?"

"Well, it's just…you and me…a middle-aged white guy with a young black girl…"

Rhea shrugs her shoulders. "No one cares."

"I know, but, back when I was your age, back when your dad and I were your age, it was something to be concerned about.

People would stare. Sometimes it led to a fight."

"I find that hard to believe sometimes." Rhea shakes her head.

"Oh, believe it. It happened."

"Just a week or so ago, daddy was telling about how he used to get into fights."

"Ask him what he was fighting about some time. Things are different now. Now, we had a black president, have black governors and mayors…"

"Yeah…it's like right now, mom and dad are at the park with a white man and a Latino man, going to watch July 4th fireworks together."

"Why aren't you there?" Grant asks. "There's some things I needed to do first."

Rhea is being evasive. "Why don't you come along?"

"Sure. It sounds like fun." Grant stops to ponder on something for a moment before continuing. "I've got some things to do around here too. How about if we meet at my house and drive over together."

Rhea nods in agreement.

The things that Rhea had to do were too unimportant to go into detail. Grant seemed to understand that they weren't really any of his business, and that's why he didn't ask.

She just needed to go home first.

Driving down Odysseus Drive toward his house gave her time to reflect on things.

Grant seems to have a number of hangups that hinder him from really enjoying life. She is glad that he accepted his invitation to take part in the July 4th festivities at the park, rather than just meet at the McDonald's because he wants some company.

On the sidewalk, she sees Brian and Stephen, who leer at her. Rhea averts her eyes, tries not to make eye contact. As she nears Grant's house, Grant rounds the corner, coming from his backyard. When Rhea pulls into his driveway, Grant gets in.

Later, as dusk arrives, Tony, Gigi and other people around them lie on blankets watching the sky. As they do, Rhea and Grant cross the grass toward them.

"Hey, here she comes," Tony announces. "Look who I found roaming the streets."

This is a good time to see how Grant handles being teased, as light as that one is.

"Grant, you missed a great meal, buddy," Perry says.

"Well, shucks," Grant responds. "It would sure beat what I ate at Mickey Ds."

Rhea likes that. It shows that he can make a joke with the best of them.

Casual conversation goes on for only a short time before the national anthem is played and everyone rises to their feet. When it's over and they all sit, the fireworks display begins.

And, it isn't long after that when Officer Miller works his way through the crowd and finds Tony.

"Mr. Carson? There's an emergency at your residence. Please come with me."

Tony looks into his face and sees that something dire has happened. The evening of fun has come to an end. There is a feeling of foreboding.

Tony and his family follow Officer Miller to their car. Seeing that something is terribly wrong motivates Grant to follow them. He drives behind them to their home to find fires burning on both the front and back lawns.

Firemen spray water in an attempt to put them out.

Tony gets out and pounds on the roof of his car with his fist.

Chapter 8

Clueless?

There is little Tony and his family can do but watch in horror as the firemen do their work. There is concern whether the smoke might make the home inhabitable. Realizing this, Grant tries to offer relief.

"Tony, I've got extra beds at my place," he says.

"Take Gigi and Rhea," Tony says softly. "I'm stayin'"

Grant pats Tony on the shoulder. "We can use Rhea's car," says Gigi.

Grant heads for Rhea's car parked along the opposite curb.

"Daddy, what's going on?" Rhea asks. "I don't know, baby," Tony answers.

"Somebody's got it in for me."

Tony stays at his home all night after Grant takes Gigi and Rhea to his house. He somberly watches Officer Miller and the firemen scour both yards looking for clues.

Officer Miller finally comes around the corner of the house from the backyard with the charred remains of two matchbooks that he got from a fireman.

"Matches and gasoline. Right?" Tony asks.

"Yes sir. The simplest time bomb in the world. Gasoline on the grass, then a lit cigarette in the matches, close the flaps, clear the area."

"Diabolical and still simple."

"We have a case opened for you, but it's not going to be easy."

"Yeah, I know. It's come down to I can't leave home," Tony tells Officer Miller as Grant listens in silence.

Officer Miller separates documents from a pad and gives one to Tony: "This is your copy of my report. My contact information is on it. Give us a call anytime."

Tony thanks the officer. After he leaves, the firemen determine that the home is, indeed, too smoke-filled to enter. They use gas masks to enter the home and open windows to allow the smoke to escape.

Grant takes Gigi and Rhea to his home where they spend the night. In the morning, Gigi and Rhea eat breakfast with him in his kitchen, a meal that Grant has prepared.

"Grant, thanks so much for letting us stay here," Gigi says.

"Anytime," Grant replies.

"You're also a very good cook," Gigi points out with emphasis.

"Thanks."

"It seems so odd to be in a new house like this," Gigi continues. "Ours was built long before we moved in."

"We've been trying to get daddy to install solar panels," Rhea explains. "It would be so much safer than using the gas and electric we got now."

"It would be safer," Grant adds. "But, it looks like whoever did it was only after the lawn."

"That seems like an awful strange way to get someone," Gigi observes.

"It's no big mystery," Rhea says. "Daddy loves his lawn."

Back at the Carson home, Tony is standing in his driveway somberly surveying the aftermath that was his lawn. Slowly, he strolls around one side of the house toward the backyard where he stops and studies the singed grass and what once was his practice putting green, now a smoldering waste. Tony angrily pounds on the corner of the house, then heads back toward the front yard. The meal he ate at the park the day before has sustained him so far, but just now, he starts to feel hunger pangs. Or is it just digestive juices irritating his stomach.

As Tony examines the grass in the front yard, Stephen and Brian stroll by. They see the charred remains and smile smugly.

"Outta sight!" Stephen exclaims.

Brian laughs. "That's what he used to say back in the day."

They both laugh as they continue on.

Tony scowls at them. He has reached the boiling point. "By God, I've had enough!" he grumbles.

Tony storms after the two boys. When Brian and Stephen see him coming, they break into a trot. Tony runs faster. He chases after the boys at high speed. The boys cross the street, but Tony crosses with them, not giving up on his pursuit.

On the opposite sidewalk, at Grant's home, Gigi, Rhea and Grant see him. "What's he doing?" Rhea asks, stunned by behavior that she has never seen before. "I fear that those boys have baited him for the last time," Grant utters with a foreboding tone.

"Tony!" Gigi calls out, not wanting to yell. "TONY!" Grant yells when he realizes that Tony is out of earshot. "Get your car," he tells Gigi. "I'll go after him."

As Gigi turns toward home, Grant and Gigi chase after Tony.

The boys put distance between them and Tony, then turn up a side street. Tony follows.

The boys cut between houses and head toward a high, wooden fence. They climb over and disappear.

Tony arrives at the same fence. He grabs the top, pulls himself over with a vengeance and disappears.

Grant and Rhea arrive in time to hear Tony groaning from the other side of the fence. When they get there and peek over, they find him tangled in rose bushes with numerous small, bloody scratches on his face and arms.

Tony is helped out of his predicament, and then finds himself having to apologize to the owners of the home and promise to pay for the roses that he just destroyed.

Embarrassed, he trudges home.

In the living room later, he sits on a chair in the middle while Gigi applies medicine to Tony's numerous scratches as Grant and Rhea watch.

"I'm sorry, but those two were really pushing my buttons," Tony says after explaining what happened.

"Makes you wish for younger days, huh?" Grant teases.

"I still think those two are the ones we're after," Tony opines.

"Maggie hates you the most," Rhea says. "I think it's her."

Tony shakes his head slowly, very puzzled by it all.

"But, you need to let the police handle it," Gigi cautions.

"Tell you what," says Grant. "How about if I go and talk to the parents? I'll be your liaison man."

"Do it," Tony utters lowly.

On the following morning, Grant makes the walk to the parents of the two boys, hoping to settle things with Tony. After some research with the local high school to learn the last names of the boys, he uses the addresses on the mailboxes to find the homes.

Grant talks with the parents, and then heads for Tony's home. His house is now inhabitable, and Tony and his family are back living there.

In the basement of Tony's home, Tony, dressed in workout clothes and still with band-aids on cuts, pounds a heavy bag hard. He is drenched in sweat.

Someone comes down the stairs. It's Grant. He sits on a bench and watches, waiting for a break to tell what he has learned.

"You're pounding that bag like a starved Attila The Hun," Grant tells Tony.

Tony stops to reply: "That's about how I feel." Tony resumes his workout.

"I talked to those boys' parents," Grant says.

"What did they say?" Tony asks.

"Well, brace yourself. The parents don't know where those boys were that night."

Tony stops his workout abruptly. This is interesting.

"So, they could be the ones?"

"Yep. The parents thought they were at the park, but then they learned they went somewhere else."

Tony grabs a towel and dries himself, then asks: "I knew it! Did you find out where they were?"

"I talked to the boys and they say they weren't anywhere in the neighborhood. But, then they were vague when I asked where they were."

Tony grabs a water bottle and drinks, then asks another question: "How come you didn't just call me and tell me all that?"

Grant shrugs his shoulders. "Just thought it would be better if I stopped by."

Tony shakes his head.

"Rhea told me you used to get into quite a few fights," Grant continues. "Fisticuffs with no rules."

"She seems to have told you a lot of things about me." Tony is suspicious. "I thought you were just dancing with her."

"Yeah, but we take breaks sometimes, and during our breaks, we chat."

Tony doesn't speak for several seconds. "There was trouble at the high school I went to. All racial." He drinks more water. "At our five-year reunion, we had a picnic. And there was this big fight."

"And you were a participant?" Grant isn't smiling nor kidding when he asks this.

"Yeah. I'm embarrassed to admit it, but, yeah, I was in on it. But, that was such a long time ago. Why would someone just suddenly pop up and start doing these things? I mean, get over it." It suddenly occurs to Tony that his past might be the incentive for the terrible things being done to him.

Grant is the one that becomes silent for several moments. "Some scars never heal."

Chapter 9

A Deadly Encounter

About a week later, in the evening after the sun goes down, Gigi watches from the kitchen as Rhea dances to sexy rumba music in the middle of the living room floor, rolling her hips as her right foot goes back and the left to the side moving in a box step.

Upstairs, in one of the bedrooms with the lights turned off, Tony stares out a window.

On the sidewalk down the street, an unknown man waits at the curb, his features indistinguishable.

In the living room, while Rhea continues to dance, Tony comes downstairs and watches her disdainfully. Gigi still watches from the kitchen.

"What are you doing?" Tony asks Rhea. "Practicing."

"Is that thing you do with your hips part of it?" Tony continues.

Rhea stops, disgusted with her father's attitude. "Yes, it is."

"Well, I don't like it."

"I can always count on you to tell me how good I'm not supposed to be." Rhea learned to fight back to her father's narrow views when she first entered her teens.

Gigi, who has been listening to the heated exchange approaches from the kitchen. "Did you come downstairs to tell her something like that?"

"No. There's somebody outside," Tony explains, regretting his comment about Rhea's dancing. "I can't help feeling like someone's watching us."

Tony goes to the window and peers out. Gigi and Rhea join him. They also see the mysterious man.

"See," Tony says. "He's up to something." "He's not doing anything," Rhea says. "I'm going to go out there and stop whatever he's up to before he does it," says Tony.

"Tony, no," Gigi moans.

Tony ignores her and leaves the house.

Outside, Tony moves toward the man. As he does this, a car stops at the curb, the man gets in and the car drives away.

Suspicious, Tony goes to the spot where the man was and watches the car's taillights disappear. A gray pickup truck drives by.

Tony pays little attention to it.

Tony continues down the sidewalk and goes by Grant's home which is dark. He stops and starts up

Grant's driveway. A security light comes on. Realizing that continuing up Grant's driveway could prove a grave error, Tony returns to the sidewalk.

Tony moves back in the direction of his own house. As he approaches Maggie's house, there is the silhouette of someone in the woods.

Tony charges up Maggie's driveway toward the woods. As he goes past her back door, Maggie is there swinging a broom that catches Tony on the back of the head.

"I'll put a stop to your shenanigans!" Maggie utters madly.

"Maggie, no! There's someone—" Tony is cut off when Maggie swings the broom again and catches him in the mouth, causing a trickle of blood that seeps from Tony's lip.

"I saw you! You were going to come in my back door!" Maggie is loud this time.

Tony says nothing further and dashes the rest of the way into the woods, a place that he has never been, and has little to no experience with.

He takes several steps forward and walks into a limb that scrapes his face. Ahead, he sees the silhouette of a man. Tony freezes.

The man moves farther into the woods. Tony follows.

In the darkness, Tony can't tell where he's walking. The dilemma makes him panic a little, and so, he quickens his pace. Suddenly, he feels a sharp pain in his legs as they collide with something hard and make him tumble to the ground. When he looks up, he sees a dead tree that is still standing and a tree stump that he fell over. There's an ugly gash that runs up and down the trunk in front of him. It occurs to him that there is a strange irony in the tree's scarred front and what he is going through.

Tony gets up and moves on, walking slowly, using his hands to feel for obstacles in his path until he comes to the edge of the trees very near a road with no curb, no sidewalk, and no street lights. He doesn't recognize where he is and there is no sign of the man.

Tony steps onto the pavement of the road.

A little confused, he looks both ways, then heads to his right.

From behind, the gray pickup truck approaches with the headlights off. Tony hears the motor and wheels around. He sees the driver's silhouette for the flash of a second. When he realizes that the truck is headed directly toward him, he lunges toward the trees, hits his head on one, and drops into bushes.

On the next morning, Tony wakes up in a hospital bed with his forehead bandaged and not understanding initially how he got there for several moments. Underneath the bandage is a large lump. Before long, Officer Miller pays him a visit, along with Gigi and Rhea.

"I haven't seen any gray pickups around, lately," Tony tells Officer Miller after a series of perfunctory questions.

"You didn't get a license number?" Officer Miller asks.

"No. But, like I said, it did look like Grant… for a second."

"Grant's out of town," Rhea says. "That's why I was practicing in the living room alone."

"Practicing what?" Officer Miller asks. "She's been getting dance lessons from our neighbor," Gigi explains.

Officer Miller jots notes before asking his next question: "Which one of you found him?" he asks the ladies.

"Mother did," Rhea answers.

"He's lucky his head's so hard," Gigi says to Officer Miller with a wide grin on her face.

"He's lucky you two found him so quick," Officer Miller states. "I spoke to the doctor. He said that if he had laid there too much longer, he might not have made it."

"Yeah, my ladies came through for me again," Tony utters.

"How much of this guy in the pickup did you see?" Officer Miller is repeating this question to see if Tony remembers anything further.

"Just a silhouette," Tony replies.

"But, Grant doesn't have any reason…" Rhea says, and then is cut off.

"Are you sure he was out of town?" Officer Miller asks.

"Yes," Rhea answers.

"Are you still going to investigate those boys, or are they out of the picture?" Tony asks Officer Miller.

"No, but it does mean a new player has entered the game," he answers.

Tony is relieved that his injury isn't so bad to require another night in the hospital. He is released later that day, and told to call if there are any complications.

When he arrives home, it makes him happier when he sees Hector and Perry busily sodding the front lawn for him. When he gets out of the car that Gigi is driving, he is immediately greeted.

"Welcome home, my friend," Hector calls out to him.

"It's good to be home," Tony replies. "We heard about what happened and came over to help," Perry says.

"When I get to doing things normal again, I owe you two some beers," Tony says to them, so grateful that he has good friends.

Tony gets the mail out of the mailbox on the curb and follows Gigi and Rhea into the house.

Inside, he sits on a sofa in the living room where sorts through the mail. He comes to a postcard. As he reads, he becomes concerned.

"Gigi," he calls out somberly.

Gigi, who was following Rhea to the kitchen, returns to see what he wants. She and Rhea are listening.

"I don't think those boys are the ones we're after," Tony continues.

Tony gives the postcard to Gigi. She reads: "''I found you, nigger. How do you like the fireworks?'" states Gigi. "It was sent from in town," she explains after examining the card.

"It's the N word," Tony says. "Those boys wouldn't write that."

Rhea enters and reads the postcard. Her jaw drops. "Aww! Who would send a card like this?"

Chapter 10

Explanations?

All is quiet under a half-moon in the evening. Lightning bugs flicker outside Tony's home as Grant's car stops at the curb.

In the living room, Tony is asleep in front of the TV set. Rhea comes downstairs, dressed for a night out. She opens the front door, and slips out quietly.

Rhea gets in Grant's car and closes the door quietly before fastening her seat belt.

"I hate sneaking out like this," she says to Grant.

"Yeah, well, if your dad is going to give you trouble, there's not much choice."

"Daddy really does love me, but he can be a pain."

"He can be a real jerk if you ask me," Grant says before shifting gears and driving away..

Inside the house, Tony pulls the living room curtain back and watches Rhea and Grant.

Grant and Rhea drive out of town to a Latino bar, one that is loud and crowded. Grant buys drinks and takes Rhea to a table where they can see the dance floor clearly. They watch other dancers participate in Rueda, a group salsa dance with partners in a circle.

"Do you know how to do that?" Rhea asks Grant loudly.

"Absolutely."

"Show me," demands Rhea without hesitation.

Grant escorts Rhea onto the dance floor where he shows her basic steps that she gets quickly. Soon, they participate, listening to steps called out in Spanish. The music and dancing get hot.

After an hour, Grant and Rhea return to their table exhausted. Both of their faces glisten in sweat. Grant continues to buy drinks at Rhea's request, some of them being club sodas in order to re-hydrate.

Later, Grant and Rhea leave the night club. When Grant brings Rhea home and pulls into the driveway, a security light above the garage comes on, followed by a hallway light inside the front door. Tony opens it to find Grant carrying Rhea in. Rhea is sleepy drunk in his arms.

"Where have you two been?" Tony asks in a very low voice.

"She wanted to check out a Latino bar," Grant explains, also in a low voice.

Grant sets Rhea down. Rhea is unstable, so, Grant holds her by the arm to keep her from falling.

"Is she alright?" Tony asks, again in a low voice.

"She's just had a little too much to drink.

How about if I carry her upstairs to bed?" Grant suggests.

"Is that all you intend to do?" Tony says with a suggestive tone, immediately drawing a scowl from Grant just before he carries her upstairs.

When Grant reaches the upstairs hallway, he is very careful about staying quiet as he carries Rhea to her bedroom, and then laying her in the bed. Rhea is asleep.

Grant stares at her for a moment, and then turns to see if Tony followed them. He did not, so, Grant bends down and kisses Rhea softly on her lips. Rhea remains asleep.

In the hallway, Tony peeks around the corner and watches.

On the following morning, Rhea begins the day with a mild hangover when she goes downstairs to breakfast. Grant left the night before, which places her in the position of dealing with her father alone.

"Rhea, I want to know what's going on between you and Grant," Tony states without hesitation as soon as he enters the kitchen.

"Nothing's going on," Rhea replies softly between bites of food.

"What happened last night ain't normal.

He's white, you're black, he's old, you're young."

"You and your old fashioned ideas!" Rhea replies vehemently. "We're just dancing! All kinds of people go out with other kinds of people! It's no big deal!"

"He carried you in," Tony tells her. "Why did he do that? And then he kissed you."

"Well, maybe he didn't want to wake you," Rhea explains, and then has to stop and think about the second half of that question. "I don't know about the kiss. I was too sleepy."

"And why didn't you tell me and your mother where you were going?"

Rhea looks at him with a sarcastic expression. She is forced to tell him why. "Because of the way you are—like right now. I just feel sorry for him because he lives alone. Besides, he's been nothing but nice to me.

He's sweet."

"Sweet, huh. How old is he anyways?

Huh? Do you know how old?"

"He's the same age you are, daddy."

"Just watch out. Sweetness comes in lots of flavors."

"You're disgusting!" Rhea finds the comment offensive.

"And another thing, I know what goes on in those Latino bars. You're not foolin' nobody." Tony isn't letting up with the badgering.

Rhea doesn't finish her breakfast.

Frustrated to the limit, she gets up and storms out of the kitchen. Just then, the front doorbell rings.

When Tony opens the door, he sees a middle-aged white man before him who smiles politely as he extends his hand.

"Mr. Carson?" he asks.

"Yes," Tony replies while shaking his hand, but quizzical about who he is and why he's at the door.

"My name is Frederick. I'm Maggie's son. From next door?"

Some of Tony's questions have been answered.

"Oh. Greetings."

"Mr. Carson, have you been having some rather mysterious things going on lately?"

"Um, yes. I'm not sure what you mean." Tony isn't sure whether to reveal everything that has happened just yet.

"Did you, for example, have a bunch of magazines show up in your mailbox that you didn't order?" Frederick asks.

"There were. Yes sir."

"Well, that was my mother behind that.

She has beginning dementia. I came here to apologize and also to inform you that she is being moved to a nursing home. I believe you may have noticed that she's seemed lost at times and then be giving you hell other times, am I correct?"

"That's putting it lightly."

"Rest assured, it's all ending," Frederick states clearly. "I just felt you should be told."

"Let me ask you something about that. Somebody set my lawn on fire and blew up my truck. Was that your mother?"

"I can't say with any degree of certainty. You see, years ago, when she was young, there were young black boys in her neighborhood that gave her all sorts of trouble. They were hoodlums basically. Ever since, she's hated black men."

"I wondered what was behind that." "Anyway, your troubles are over. Good day, sir." Frederick shakes Tony's hand again, and then leaves very abruptly.

Tony feels like a weight has been lifted from his shoulders. Some of the trouble he has been having is now over, but not everything. There's still a mystery to be solved.

Tony's issues with Rhea and her escapade with Grant the night before is put on the back burner for now. He still doesn't understand why Grant allowed her to drink so much alcohol, but maybe he didn't realize what she was doing. Tony wasn't there, he realizes. Maybe that's what happened.

Tony grabs a beer from the fridge and goes to the back yard where he sits in a chair under the shade of an eave. He stares idly at the woods as he thinks. Faintly, he hears men's voices, a dock door open, followed by a truck's engine, and a forklift.

It suddenly occurs to Tony that he has never heard these noises before. Why is that? He's never sat in the back yard at this time of day. Perhaps that's the reason.

Tony gets up, crosses his bare lawn now covered in sods of grass and fertilizer, and enters the woods.

Unlike the last time he was here, it isn't dark and Tony can see where he's going. He finds a footpath and follows it toward the noises until he comes to the back of the abandoned shopping center and watches men on a loading dock load display furniture into a truck.

Tony emerges from the trees and heads toward the loading dock. From there, he sees a long row of loading docks and windows of abandoned retail stores, then turns and looks toward his house, barely noticeable through the trees. Realizing that he has something significant, he pulls a cell phone from a pants pocket, punches buttons and; puts it to his ear.

"Officer Miller? Tony Carson here. How ya' doin'?" Tony stops to listen to Officer Miller before explaining. "Say, on that bullet that came through our bedroom, have you checked out this old shopping center on the other side of the woods?" Again, he stops to listen before speaking. "You have?" Tony listens one last time to an explanation before saying goodbye and hanging up.

Did he get the answer he wanted?

Tony goes to the men on the dock, just now noticing that they all wear hardhats. He singles out one that seems to be in charge.

"Is Grant here?" Tony asks bluntly. "Not yet," the man replies. "If you go around front, you might catch him coming in."

"Fine. I'll do that."

Tony makes the long walk to the end of the building and arrives at the front of a closed retail store just as Grant arrives. When Grant sees him, he rolls his window down.

"Tony, watcha doin' here?" Grant asks. "Felt like doin' some fishin'," is Tony's reply.

Grant gets out of his car with a hardhat in his hand. "I have to work today. Sorry, buddy."

"I heard people working and came over to have a look," Tony states with a chuckle. "Tell me something, are you over here much?"

"Oh, a couple times a week. I've got other projects outside of town."

"How many people you got?"

"You mean in the company?" Grant is puzzled by the nature of the questions.

"No, here."

"It depends. Guys need days off…about ten usually."

"Are your people the only ones over here?"

"During the day. Don't know about night.

Why are you asking?"

"I got trouble. You know that. The magazine thing got cleared up, but there's still the other shit."

"Magazines? I don't understand…" Grant continues to be puzzled.

"Never mind." If Grant is the one, he doesn't seem to understand what all has happened, Tony thinks to himself. Either that or he's putting up a great act.

"I'd let you come in and look around, but I only have one hat," Grant explains. "You can't be in there without one."

"I know that."

"Say, I've got something for you."

Grant opens his car and gets a pair of tickets that he hands to Tony. Tony reads them.

"A dance contest."

Tony returns through the woods on the same footpath that he followed earlier, impressed by the progress his daughter has made with her dancing. He keeps glancing at the tickets. A dance contest. He's never been to one.

Halfway through the woods, he glances to his right and notices a campfire and a tent through the trees. He decides to turn and investigate. This is another thing that he's never noticed before.

Soon, he comes into view of a small camp with two male transients. Tony stops. The transients don't see him. Tony wheels around and quietly heads toward home. This is a new development. Perhaps those two men are behind the chaos.

Chapter 11

The Dance Competition

It is a warm, humid evening when Tony and Gigi attend Rhea's dance competition. Dressed in a sharp suit, but without a tie, Tony escorts Gigi toward a large hotel and conference center, among a crowd of people dressed similar to them. Tony's coat is open and Gigi notices.

"Why didn't you put on a tie?" Gigi asks. "I don't even know how to tie a tie," Tony replies. "By the time I got it on, we'd be late." "Then, I guess, going without is the thing to do."

"I hate dressing up," Tony states. "You want to fit in, don't you?" "Not particularly," Tony sighs.

Tony and Gigi come to a long line with their tickets in hand. When they finally show their tickets, they take programs, and enter a huge arena. They make their way to steps that lead upward into the grandstands until they reach the last row all of the way at the top.

"It sure is a long way from the action up here," Tony says.

Soon after they're seated, dance couples enter the arena from the far side. An announcer calls out unintelligibly over a PA system.

"Can you tell what he's saying?" Tony asks Gigi lowly.

"Uh-uh," replies Gigi.

Other people in the grandstand have to refer to their program to sort out who is who.

"Do you see Rhea and Grant?" Tony asks. "No." Gigi says this as she squints at the contestants. "Oh, yes, there they are." Gigi points them out.

After more unintelligible words from the announcer, the dancers take position, foxtrot music plays and the competition begins.

"Ohhhh, aren't they wonderful?" Gigi utters.

After several minutes go by, the music and dancers stop and line up on one side of the dance floor. More unintelligible comments come from the announcer, then, dancers are eliminated. Grant and Rhea are among them.

"What happened?!" Tony asks with his mouth agape.

"I don't think they made it," answers Gigi. "Damn!"

"Don't worry about it. They dance again later." Gigi indicates the program in her hand.

Tony and Gigi continue to watch many dance competitions, enthralled by the numerous amazing dancers. When Grant and Rhea appear in one later, they are further thrilled when they win third place, dancing the same Rumba that they saw Rhea practicing in the living room.

After it's all over, they wait for Grant and Rhea in the lobby of the hotel, who arrive with wide grins on their faces and a trophy in hand.

"There come the dance pros," Tony says to them.

"Not bad for a first try, don't you think?" Grant asks.

"Are you proud of me now?" Rhea asks her father.

"Am I proud? Am I proud? I'm so proud, I'm buying supper," Tony announces.

Tony escorts the group to the hotel dining room, crowded from all of the people attending the dance contest, where they sit at a table with the trophy in the middle and waiting to place their orders.

"Grant kept talking me through it all the way around. I would've been lost without him," Rhea tells her mother after being asked how they did it.

"Now you can take that trophy and show it to the dance team coach at school. He'll have to put you on the team," Gigi says.

As this conversation is going on, Tony and Grant are involved in another topic, one that deals with a more serious topic.

"I never expected to see hobos way out here in the 'burbs'," Tony tells Grant.

"Oh, they can be found about anywhere nowadays," says Grant.

"You never noticed them before?" Tony asks.

"I never enter a woods," Grant explains. "You can catch things nobody's ever heard of."

"You never…? I thought I…" Tony is thinking about the silhouetted man he saw in the woods at night that he thought was Grant. He realizes that he may be wrong.

"I never what?" Grant asks.

"Never mind." Tony has to change the subject. "Let's get some champagne.

Where's the waiter?"

Meals are ordered and served amid more casual conversation that remains pleasant until later when Tony excuses himself to go use the men's lavatory. While he's using the urinal, Grant enters and does the same at an adjoining urinal. Tony stares at Grant, then clears his throat. There's something else on his mind that he has decided to bring up now.

"The other night…" he begins.

Grant is daydreaming and doesn't hear him at first.

"Huh?" Grant finally answers.

"The other night, I saw you kiss my daughter," Tony says.

Grant says nothing as Tony finishes and washes his hands at the sink.

"After tonight, it ends," Tony adds.

"Your daughter's a grown woman, buddy," Grant replies forcefully. "That's none of your business."

Tony grabs a paper towel and dries his hands as he gets near Grant. "You stay away from her." Tony throws the paper towel away and leaves in a huff.

Tony's comment to Grant has no visible effect on ensuing events. Grant takes Rhea home in his car, parking at the curb in front as Tony and Gigi arrive in their vehicle. They pull into the driveway as Rhea gets out of Grant's car, exhausted from the long day.

Grant remains in his car with the motor running as Tony and Gigi get out of theirs. Tony's clothes are unkempt, a product of another long, sweaty day. Both he and Gigi are totally pooped.

"Thanks for the drinks, man," Tony says to Grant after an uncomfortable silence. His comments in the men's lavatory were a waste of time and energy, he sees.

Grant is very alert, unlike the others. "You're very welcome. A stupor a day keeps the bed bugs away." Grant has tried to smooth over the angst caused by Tony's comments to him in the hotel lavatory by buying drinks. So, far, he thinks, it's working.

Tony looks at Grant curiously as Grant grimly heads toward home. Tony moves toward the front door. Rhea digs in her purse looking for her house keys while Gigi waits.

"I can't find my key," Rhea mutters.

"I got mine," Tony says as he unlocks the front door.

Saying little to one another, Tony and his family trudge upstairs.

Rhea goes to her bedroom and shuts the door. Tony and Gigi do the same with their bedroom. All parties want nothing more than to go to bed. All is quiet.

Chapter 12

The Last Blow

After a few hours go by, Tony awakens.

He's not sure why, but he lies in bed listening. He normally sleeps throughout the night without waking.

Tony listens closely for noises, but hears none. Then, he starts to wonder if someone might have been in the house, so he gets up and goes downstairs.

When he reaches the ground floor, he tries the front door and finds that it's locked. He's glad that someone remembered to lock it. Next, he goes to the curtains in the front window and peeks out. There's no one outside. The street is empty.

Satisfied that there's no one lurking outside, Tony heads for the kitchen where he stubs his toe on a chair in the darkness and suppresses reacting vocally. Limping to the basement door, he opens the basement door and looks down the steps into the darkness. He hears nothing.

Tony's next move is to try the door knob on the back door. It too is locked. The house is safe and he doesn't know what he heard, so, he goes back upstairs and climbs back in bed. Not longer after, he is asleep.

A dramatic change takes place in just a few hours. When Tony awakens at his usual time, he grasps his forehead in pain.

Something is off. He sniffs the air, then looks at Gigi. She isn't moving. Tony can't tell whether she's breathing.

"Gigi," he calls out softly at first, and then: "GIGI!?"

He jostles her gently, and then with force. No response. Tony starts to suspicion what is going on, so he heads for Rhea's room, sniffing the air as he goes.

In Rhea's bedroom, he finds the same thing. Rhea is unresponsive.

Fighting a blinding headache, Tony carries Rhea downstairs and outside where he lays her on the lawn. Next is Gigi. He climbs the stairs, wearing down quickly, but unwilling to give in. When he carries Gigi down, he finds her heavier than he expected. But, he will not drop her. Fighting through pain, he gets her outside and lays her next to Rhea. He tries to shake both of them gently and they stir a little.

The next thing is to call for help. Tony races back inside the house and returns with his cell phone. He punches buttons and puts the phone to his ear.

"Yeah, I've got two women at my residence that are semi-conscious," Tony begins upon being asked what his emergency is. "13927 Odysseus Drive. Outside on the lawn."

Tony hangs up and grasps his forehead in pain again. Grant pulls up to the curb in his sports car and rolls the window down.

"What's wrong?" Grant asks, very concerned.

"I think we've got a gas leak," Tony replies. "They're both barely conscious."

"Is EMS coming?"

"I called," Tony says.

"I can get them to the hospital faster," Grant suggests.

Tony stops to think for a second. "Let's do it."

Grant gets out of his car and helps Tony transfer the ladies to his car.

"I don't have room for you," says Grant. "Just go. I'll wait for the ambulance." Grant says nothing more. He gets into his car and speeds away.

Minutes later, two ambulances arrive. A mimed conversation takes place and the ambulances leave. Tony remains alone as sprinklers come on in the yards around him.

Not long after, when the police arrive, which means Officer Miller is there supervising a team with gas masks who enter Tony's house, Tony uses his cell phone to check on his ladies.

"Yes, I would like to check on the status of two patients there," Tony says after calling the nearest hospital, assuming that they were taken there. "Gigi and Rhea Carson." Tony becomes concerned when he hears the answer. "Not there? Are you sure?"

Tony listens to the receptionist who checks again for him. "No record." He listens once again for a brief moment. "I'm coming over."

Tony hangs up. As he does, a police officer with a gas mask confers with Officer Miller, then Officer Miller approaches Tony.

"Give it a few hours and you can go back in," Officer Miller tells Tony. "It looks like somebody's been in your house fiddling with your furnace."

"Last night, I thought I heard something," Tony mentions.

"Are you alright?" Officer Miller asks as he studies Tony's eyes.

"My head's a lot clearer than it was."

"You should get checked out."

"Later. Right now, I have to find my wife and daughter." Tony is starting to become anxious about the whereabouts of his family.

Tony jumps in the closest vehicle, starts it up and backs into the street where he speeds away. He makes it to the same hospital that he just called, hoping that Gigi and Rhea might have arrived while he was on his way. Tony parks and hurries in.

Inside the door, Tony sees a white-haired elderly woman seated behind a desk. She's probably retired and volunteers here, Tony realizes. That's the first person to ask.

"We have no one by those names," she tells Tony after he asks the same questions that he asked over the phone.

Tony is very puzzled. "This is the closest hospital. Where else would people who inhaled toxic fumes be taken?"

"This would be the most logical place if it's the closest," the woman says.

"What would have happened to them? Was there an accident?" Tony tries to go through a list of possibilities that could have happened.

"None that we're aware of," the woman answers.

Tony stops to ponder for several moments before making his next move. "Okay.

Thanks. I'll have to do some checking." He wheels around and leaves the building.

Tony returns home in just a few minutes. When he gets out of his car, he tries to make a call on his cell phone as he stands on the front lawn where new grass barely sticks out of the ground. When he punches buttons and puts the phone to his ear, he gets a surprise.

"Disconnected?! What the…?!"

As the lawn sprinklers come on, Tony is puzzled and fuming. He enters his house and goes to his kitchen where he prepares breakfast. He's going to need nutrition for this day. He sniffs the air and is relieved when nothing happens. It smells fresh and clean.

Tony sits down and starts to drink a glass of orange juice when the wall phone rings.

Tony picks up the receiver and puts it to his ear.

"Hello?" Tony listens, but there is silence. "Who is this?" he asks. This time someone speaks to him.

"How the hell do you know that?" he demands, then slams the receiver back onto the phone. "Goddamn it! Who's doing this?!" Tony didn't recognize the voice. It sounded like someone disguising it.

Tony wolfs down his breakfast. When he finishes, he rushes from the house and gets into his car. After backing into the street, Tony drives the short distance to Grant's home to see if he's back. Somehow, he feels that the answer to this mystery will be found here.

When Tony pulls into Grant's driveway and gets out, he senses that something is different. He can't put a finger on it, but something isn't right. He goes to the front door and rings the doorbell. There is no answer. Irritated, Tony glances in the front window and notices that there is no furniture.

Tony goes to the window and looks closer, then goes around to the driveway. He goes to the kitchen window, peers in, and again sees that there is no furniture.

The next move is to go to a basement window where he peers in, and again, there is no furniture.

Perplexed and very concerned, Tony calls on his cell phone.

"Officer Miller? Tony Carson here," he begins. "Say…" He stops to listen to a question from the policeman. "Clean bill. I'm fine. This Grant Ziegler, his house is empty. I think he just up and moved out." And then there is one more question from Officer Miller that Tony replies to. "Yeah. Something's up with him."

Tony hangs up and decides to go home. Pieces of the puzzle are jumbled like a large jigsaw puzzle. He needs to take some time to organize his thoughts.

When Tony returns home, he gets a beer out of the fridge and sits at the kitchen table drinking it while he thinks. A clue suddenly occurs to him.

"The same age," he mutters to himself. Tony takes his beer with him to his and Gigi's bedroom upstairs where he locates his high school yearbook in the closet. He takes it to the bed where he sits and flips through the photos until he comes to Grant's picture.

Tony's mind travels back to an afternoon in the high school gymnasium where an unsuspecting, teenage Grant Ziegler crosses amid a sparse crowd of teenagers. Teenage Tony Carson runs up behind him, swings his fist and slugs Grant in the temple, knocking him to the floor, and then kicking and pounding the helpless boy.

"Son-of-a-bitch!" Tony exclaims to himself.

Tony's mind drifts into the past again when he was twenty-two and attending the five-year high school reunion at a park. A big fight erupts among young black and white men. Tony swings his fist and knocks out a white man. He goes wild as he wades into the others.

Tony's past is the motive. He can see that now. But, for now he can only wait, so he goes downstairs and gets several bottles of beer that he takes back to his bedroom where he can lie in bed and drink. He puts his cell phone on a nightstand next to the bed next to a landline phone and a digital clock.

The beers make Tony sleepy drunk until he loses sense of time and falls asleep. And then, the landline phone rings. It wakens him. The clock reads five PM. Has the entire day gone by? He answers the phone.

"Hello?" Tony begins with caution in his voice.

"Hey, buddy, how do you like the headache I gave you?" the voice asks.

Tony realizes, even with the buzz from the beer, that only a couple of people know that he had a headache from the gas.

"What'd you do with my family?" Tony demands.

"Your family's just fine," the voice replies. "I want to talk to one of them."

"Not tonight."

"I know who you are now…Grant," Tony states. "I found you in my yearbook. I remember."

"You remember what?" Grant is being evasive.

"You know what I mean. It must've taken a long time to figure out where I live."

There is a long silence while Tony waits for an answer and doesn't get one.

"Was finding me planned all these years, or was it just luck you moved into the same neighborhood?" Tony inquires.

There is another very long pause before Grant answers: "I never went to any of the reunions because of you. I never knew why. I didn't do anything to you. Why…?"

"Why?" answers Tony. "Because you were white. That's all."

"For years and years, I dreamed of the day I would catch up with you." Grant is starting to reveal his feelings.

"Well, when does it end, man? I can't go back and do it all over. I was a kid. Just a stupid, immature kid."

"If you weren't such an idiot with me and Rhea, it wouldn't be still happening. It ends when I say it ends."

"You got my wife and my daughter. You got me. The other shit don't matter. They do. And when I catch up with you…eventually I'll catch up with you, and when I do, your head is mine!" Aggressive is the only way Tony knows to handle when he is being threatened.

Grant hangs up.

Tony has no doubt where the call came from. He slams the receiver onto the phone, tears down the stairs and out through the door. He gets into his vehicle, starts the engine and backs into the street from where he burns rubber when he steps on the accelerator, then speeds away.

Tony arrives at the abandoned shopping center in just a few minutes, skidding to a halt next to Grant's car. Tony knew that he might find it here. When he gets out, he looks into that vehicle and sees that it's packed with luggage.

Tony searches the building, looking for a way in. When he goes to the side of the structure, he finds a side door that is unlocked. When he gets it open and looks at the lock mechanism, he sees that it's broken.

Inside, the place is totally dark. Tony pulls out a small flashlight on his key chain that he turns on. The store is very musty, with dust everywhere. He spots an opening in the corner.

When he gets closer, he sees that it's not a door, but a crack in the wall that is big enough for him to slide through.

The next large room is another abandoned store. There, Tony sees the gray pickup truck. When he tries to fishes for his cell phone in his pants pocket, he realizes that he left it at home.

"Damn!" he utters.

Tony spots a .22 rifle in the bed of the truck and takes it. Now he has a weapon. His flashlight reveals another door in the corner. When he moves to that door, he hears movement from somewhere. He's not sure where.

The next empty store is much bigger than the others. When Tony enters, he sees several poles, many counters, display racks and, dressing rooms. It is also very dark.

From swinging doors that lead to a back storage area, Tony sees a light. He turns and walks in that direction slowly. When he reaches the doors, he peeks through the window and sees Gigi and Rhea in an office cubicle, bound and gagged on the carpet, their heads on pillows. The office area is slightly illuminated by light from covered windows, albeit very little at night.

From the darkness behind, a forklift with headlights on comes at him. Tony wheels and lifts the rifle. The forklift prongs shatter it as Tony dives to the floor with a loud grunt. The forklift whizzes by. Grant drives wearing a hardhat and work gloves. Grant swings the forklift around for another try.

"Hey, buddy, who's the monster here?! Huh?! You or me?!" Grant yells out at Tony.

"You've got to stop this, man!" Tony utters in a high pitch.

Grant drives the forklift straight at Tony. Tony rolls out of the way. Grant spins the forklift around again, ready to attack as Tony jumps to his feet and darts behind a pole.

When Grant drives at him again, Tony goes around the pole, grabs Grant by the sleeve and drags him from the forklift.

Grant kicks him in the groin. Tony doubles over in pain.

Grant gets back on the forklift, swings it around in a circle and comes at Tony once more. Tony, in agony, turns and runs. He darts behind a display counter.

Grant rams the counter and drives it toward Tony. The counter becomes impaled on the front blades.

Tony dashes away into a dark corner where he spots a large pile of dirt that has probably been swept there by an employee. Nearby is an upright fan. A idea comes to him.

Grant comes at Tony again with the forklift. Before taking off again, Tony flips the fan on.

Tony runs around a stack of pallets, picks one up and slings it at Grant. The pallet crashes into the front of the forklift. Grant ducks.

Tony rushes Grant, grabs his arm and tries to pull him off of the seat. As one of Grant's hands is jerked from the steering wheel, Grant uses his hardhat with his other hand to pound on Tony's hand and face.

Tony pulls away, taking one of Grant's gloves off with him. He then runs back toward the fan, grabs a shovel, scoops up the dirt and waits.

Grant heads toward him on the forklift.

Tony waits until he gets close, then throws the dirt into the wind from the fan. The dirt sprays all over Grant's face, body and bare hand.

Grant is frantic.

"Nooooo! no, no, no, no! Get it off me!

Get it off!" he screams.

Grant claws at his hand and face. He turns the forklift and drives away, disappearing into the darkness.

Tony waits a few seconds to see if Grant returns, pretty certain that he won't, then heads for the cubicle where he found Gigi and Rhea.

When he unties them, they become groggy when they try to stand up. Their legs had become too stiff. Tony has to help them.

"I don't know if he'll be back, but we gotta' hurry," Tony states. "Can you make it?"

"A little woozy, but getting better," Rhea says with a squeaky voice, raw from inhaling dust.

The trio make it to Tony's vehicle safely where they find that Grant's car is gone.

When they get in, Tony starts the engine. "Daddy, why was he after you so bad?" Rhea asks.

"I did something to him way back in high school. He just never forgot it."

"Did you hurt him?" Rhea asks.

"Yeah," Tony answers as he drives away. "But, why?" Rhea continues.

"It's the whole black and white thing," Gigi replies.

"Grant liked black girls," Tony explains.

"I thought you said you weren't into girls," Rhea says.

"I lied, kind of. We both liked the same girl."

"Grant was a white boy who liked black girls and you beat him up because he liked a girl you liked. Daddy, how could you?!" Rhea asks pleadingly. "Didn't you ever want to find him and say you're sorry?!"

"No, I never did."

"It's terrible!" says Rhea.

"That's the biggest crime," Gigi adds.

Tony turns onto Odysseus Drive and goes to their home. He has to make a stop. "I forgot my phone. As soon as we get inside, we have to call the police and then the hospital after that."

Tony escorts his wife and daughter to the front door which he unlocks. Inside, he tells them to wait while he goes upstairs. Rhea and Gigi wait by the front door, both a little nauseous. Tony returns with his cell phone. He starts to punch buttons and then hesitates.

"Aren't you calling the police?" Rhea asks him.

Tony stares at the phone for several seconds before answering. "If I were Grant, I'd do the same damn thing."

"You should call," Gigi tells him.

"I was just wondering if there's a statute of limitations on battery charges." Tony is worried about what he did to Grant all those many years ago. "Maybe he left town. But, this phone wasn't working when I tried it earlier. I'll take it with me and figure it our later."

Tony closes his phone and they head for the car. He has to get them to the hospital to have them checked out.

The drive to the hospital in the predawn is slow and easy for Tony, relieved that he has his family back safely. There probably is nothing to be concerned about regarding their health based on how strong they seem when they talk to him on the way there, but it's better to go through with the procedure.

When they arrive at the hospital as the sun rises in the east, Tony has to park far away from the entrance in the nearly filled parking lot.

The walk to the hospital entrance is peaceful in the coolness of the new day. Inside, they confer with the same older lady that Tony met the day before.

After a phone call by the elderly woman, a nurse arrives to escort Gigi and Rhea to examining rooms.

"It looks like we'll be here for a few hours," Gigi tells Tony.

"It looks like," Tony replies. "I tell you what, I'll go grab some breakfast somewhere and come back for you, okay?"

Gigi and Rhea wave at Tony as they follow the nurse, still not feeling well. Tony turns and heads for the door.

Outside, as Tony approaches his vehicle, Grant's car follows. Tony never sees him when he unlocks his door. Grant's car stops. Grant gets out with his iron bat in hand.

"Hey, you son-of-a-bitch!" Grant spews out with venom.

Tony turns. Grant swings, striking Tony across the bridge of his nose. Tony goes down. Blood oozes from his nose, but he is alive.

Grant goes to his car, gets in and drives away.

THE END